YAEL WALFISH, LCSW

Menucha
FOR MENUCHA

ILLUSTRATED BY MIRA SIMON

MENUCHA PUBLISHERS

Menucha Publishers, Inc.
Text © 2022 by Yael Walfish
Illustrations © 2022 by Mira Simon
Typeset and designed by the Virtual Paintbrush
All rights reserved

ISBN 978-1-61465-567-1
Library of Congress Control Number: 2021943442

Published and distributed by:
Menucha Publishers, Inc.
1235 38th Street
Brooklyn, NY 11218
Tel/Fax: 718-232-0856
www.menuchapublishers.com
sales@menuchapublishers.com

Printed in China

THIS BOOK BELONGS TO

_____

_____

ONCE UPON A TIME, there was a girl named Menucha.

Menucha was seven years old. She had brown pigtails and big blue eyes. She loved to bounce for hours on her pogo stick, and she jumped rope longer than anybody.

There was always something she wanted — and she wanted it so much! At school, she asked her teacher, "Is it snack time yet? Can we go outside for recess now? Can we have a prize?"

But sometimes Menucha didn't get what she wanted. When that happened, a big storm cloud appeared over her head. The room

BOOMED

with thunder. Raindrops poured down her cheeks!

The whole neighborhood heard the **BOOMS** and said, "There goes Menucha!" They shut their windows so the storm couldn't come into their houses.

The storm cloud was so scary! It

BANGED

against the doors. It blew things around the room. Menucha's toys were strewn across the floor. All of her dolls had lost an eye or an ear.

Poor Menucha. She had no peace. She had no *menucha*!

One day Menucha woke up too early. Another day she woke up too late. One night she wanted the window open, but her sisters wanted it closed. So many troubles made the

STORM CLOUD

burst, with raining tears and thundering yells.

Once Menucha started wailing, there was no stopping her. The cloud got darker and thicker over her head. Nothing her parents said or did made it go away. Not talking. Not begging or pleading. Not even sending Menucha to her room.

Menucha cried, she wailed, she threatened. There was simply no *menucha* with Menucha's storm cloud around!

Menucha's parents wanted to chase away that horrible cloud. Her mother spoke to Menucha's teacher.
She spoke to a counselor in a fancy office. She spoke to Menucha's aunts and grandmother.

But nothing helped. Nothing at all! The cloud followed Menucha everywhere.

Menucha's parents didn't give up.
When the cloud wasn't around,
Menucha was cute and fun.
She sparkled with new ideas for
games and make-believe. How could
they help her stay calm?

One day, Menucha's parents came
up with a plan. They decided to
stop trying to chase the cloud away.
Instead, they would let Menucha
figure out how to do it herself.

Menucha wasn't sure she liked this new idea. She didn't like it when her parents talked about her storm cloud. Why couldn't they talk to her when the storm cloud came?
Did they plan to leave her all alone with it?

She squeezed her eyes shut and balled her hands into fists.
She felt the air over her head gather into a cloud.

Then Menucha's mother said that they were having fish for supper. Menucha hated fish. Now the cloud grew **BIG** and **DARK**.

It started to thunder and rain!

Her parents didn't say a word.

Menucha was swept up in the **STORM**. She lay on the floor and kicked. She tore up an art project. She jumped and screamed.

Her parents didn't even look at her. Menucha didn't like this, not one bit.

"You're ignoring me!" she cried.

Nobody answered. One by one, Menucha's parents and sisters quietly left the room.

After what seemed like forever,
Menucha stopped screaming.
The cloud got

SMALLER

and

SMALLER

and started to drift away.

When it was gone, Menucha's family
came back into the room.

"Wow, Menucha! You stopped
screaming!" her mother said.
"Now tell us, what was
bothering you?"

Menucha started to scream again. The cloud came rushing back!

Her family moved as fast as a Hatzalah rescue crew. They turned on music and began to sing. You couldn't hear the thunder and wailing over the singing, so finally Menucha gave a few deep, shivery breaths and calmed down.

The cloud turned into **little wisps**, and…

Whoosh! It floated away.

Her family cheered.

Soon Menucha's family began to notice whenever she found ways to calm herself down.

When Menucha was calm, she could say what was bothering her. If her sister looked over her shoulder while she was doing homework, she said, "It bothers me when you stand so close." If her mother asked her to clean her room, she said, "I want to go play now. Can I clean up later?"

The cloud came less and less. Now Menucha could see the clear blue sky! She was happy and calm. Her family was glad they didn't have to live with a **STORM CLOUD** all the time.

And Menucha was still the same fun person. Now she had more friends. Her teachers loved her. When Menucha was around, the sun shone.

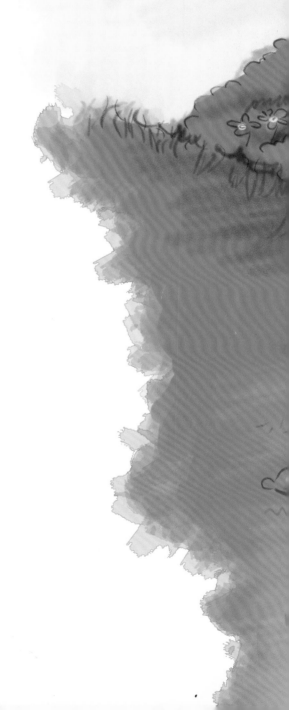

And the **STORM CLOUD**? Menucha had no more use for him. So he packed his bags and moved to Florida to be with his cousins Hurricane Harvey and Tropical Storm Tillie.

Menucha's family waved goodbye.

After all, their lives were

SUNNY

now too.

A NOTE TO PARENTS

Sometimes children get swept up in very strong feelings and don't know how to deal with them. They may seem furious, out of control, or inconsolable. But they can learn to be clear about what they need and to diminish the outbursts of negative energy.

The Nurtured Heart Approach™ is an internationally acclaimed approach to *chinuch* that offers methods for handling intense children. Children can learn to reset themselves, calm down, and stop tantruming. As parents learn to help their children reset, children can rechannel their energies into constructive pursuits and focus on the positive. Once they calm down, their true, lovable personalities and hidden talents begin to emerge and shine.

ACKNOWLEDGMENTS

With gratitude to Hashem for helping me reach this point. May all children and families find their *menucha*.

Naftoli, you are coauthor, partner, and anchor in this shared journey. You've encouraged me to follow my dreams at home and beyond.

To our children: Abba and I are so proud of each of you and how you have developed your *kochos*. We are honored to be your parents.

Ima, Abba, Mom, and Dad: You have supported us as a couple and a family and encouraged every step, watching each presentation, reading each draft, and sharing your clarity.

Barbara, you took each word and created a tapestry that can reach the hearts of children and help them connect with their spark.

Celeste, you've shared your wisdom and experience. I am ever grateful for your friendship and mentorship.

Esther, you helped me patiently through this brand-new process. Mira, you brought Menucha to life. She has joy, fun, and is full of spunk.

And so many more that I haven't named... Sisters-in-law, cousins, friends, and all the parents and teachers I have met with in-person and online, you each inspire me. I can't wait to hear the success stories from this book!

Yael

ABOUT THE AUTHOR

YAEL WALFISH, LCSW, is a therapist in private practice. She and her husband, Naftoli Walfish, LCSW, have trained individuals, families, and organizations in the Nurtured Heart Approach, both in the US and abroad. They have been featured in *Mishpacha* magazine, *Binah* magazine, and other Jewish publications, and have presented Power Talks at Torah Umesorah and Nefesh International conventions, as well as many other venues. Yael can be reached through CenterForGreatness.com.

ABOUT THE ILLUSTRATOR

From a young age, **MIRA SIMON** dreamed of illustrating children's books. She has tried her hand at a variety of mediums and styles of art, but she is happiest when drawing for children. Mira lives in Telz Stone, Israel, with her husband and children, who provide her with ample inspiration for her drawings.